The New House

Contents

Pioneer Valley Educational Press, Inc.

ISBN 9781584532293

Chapter 1
A Sad Dog

Pickles looked around. Why had Danny, Amy, Mom, and Dad packed up all of their things? Why were they moving everything into this strange house?

A moving truck came
and took everything away.
Everyone climbed in the car and
followed the truck to the new house.

Pickles didn't like the new house.
The kitchen was different.

Her dog dish was in a different
place in the new kitchen.
Pickles liked where her dog dish
was in the old kitchen.

Pickles sat on Danny's bed.
It was the same bed,
but it was different!
Pickles liked Danny's old room.
She liked where the bed
was in Danny's *old* room!

The furniture in the living room
was the same furniture,
but it looked different.

Pickles was very sad.

She lay down to take a nap.

She thought, "Why did we move?"

Chapter 2
Running Away

"What's wrong with Pickles?"
Danny asked his mom.

"I think Pickles is sad because we
moved," said Danny's mother.
"I think she misses our old house."

"But this is a great house!"
said Danny. "I like my new room
and the big yard!"

"I know," said his mother.
"I hope Pickles will like it soon, too."

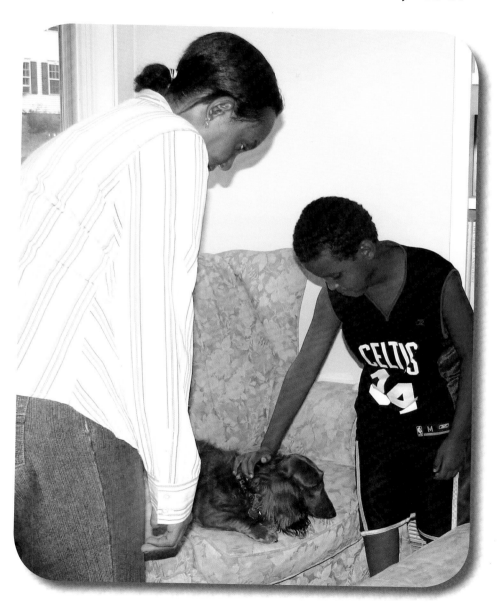

Danny kept trying
to get Pickles to play.
"Come on, Pickles," said Danny.
"Let's play!"

But Pickles didn't want to play.
Pickles was sad.
She was a sad dog.
All she wanted to do was go home.

Pickles decided to run away.
She would go back
to the old house.

She waited and waited
for a chance to get away.
Finally, someone left the door open,
and out she went.
Pickles ran down the hill
to the street.
No one was watching!
She was going home.

Pickles walked and walked.

The old house was far away.

Pickles was hot and tired,
but she didn't stop.

She kept on walking.

Finally, Pickles could see
her old house.
There was her wonderful,
wonderful house.

Pickles walked up the driveway.
She was so happy to see her house!

Chapter 3
Home Again

Pickles stood on the porch looking around.

Everything about the house looked the same.
But something was wrong.

Pickles thought and thought.
"What is going on here?
What is wrong with the house?"

"The house is the same.
But where are Danny and Amy?"
wondered Pickles.
"Where are Mom and Dad?"

The house Pickles loved
was here, but the people Pickles
loved were not!

Pickles thought and thought
about this. Then she turned
and began walking
back to the new house.

Danny was sitting on
the front steps of the new house.
He looked up and saw Pickles.

"Pickles!" he said.
"Where have you been?"

"Woof, woof!" barked Pickles.
She was tired,
but she was also happy.
She was finally home!